HAUNTED STATES
of
AMERICA

TRAPPED
— in —
ROOM 217

Book design by Sarah Taplin
Illustrations by Maggie Ivy

Published in the United States by Jolly Fish Press, an imprint of North Star Editions, Inc.

First Edition
First Printing, 2018

This is a work of fiction. Names, characters, places, and incidents are either the product of the author's imagination or are used fictitiously, and any resemblance to actual persons living or dead, business establishments, events, or locales is entirely coincidental.

Library of Congress Cataloging-in-Publication Data (pending)
978-1-63163-216-7 (paperback)
978-1-63163-215-0 (hardcover)

Jolly Fish Press
North Star Editions, Inc.
2297 Waters Drive
Mendota Heights, MN 55120
www.jollyfishpress.com

Printed in the United States of America

HAUNTED STATES
of
AMERICA

TRAPPED
— in —
ROOM 217

THOMAS KINGSLEY TROUPE

Illustrated by Maggie Ivy

JOLLY
FiSH
PRESS

Mendota Heights, Minnesota

CHAPTER 1

NIGHT CALL

Jayla Walters was fast asleep and dreaming about math. She was sitting in an empty classroom at Wilson Middle School. Her teacher, Mr. Pullman, was sitting at his desk, squinting at the monitor on his laptop. She didn't know why, but she had to hurry. A quick glance at the clock told her it was almost thirteen o'clock. It didn't seem weird to her that there was a thirteen at the top of the white-and-black timepiece above the dry-erase board, nor did Jayla take much notice at what was blowing around outside the windows.

Papers. Everywhere, covering the parking lot and the hedges lining the property. A swirling mass of work-sheets and homework.

Focus, Jayla told herself. She wasn't good at taking tests and knew Mr. Pullman was probably wondering what her problem was. With a tap of the eraser, she looked down at the math problems in front of her. Her eyes glazed over when she realized her test wasn't made up of just one sheet anymore. There was a stack of at least thirty papers waiting for her attention.

Even though I haven't even started, I can do this, Jayla thought. *Even if everyone is already done, I can do this*. Distracted again, Jayla looked around the room. All the empty desks seemed different, almost like they were slowly melting. Where was everyone?

"What's the capital of North Dakota, Jayla?" Mr. Pullman asked. Jayla looked over toward the front of the room to see Mr. Pullman wearing a cowboy hat. Also, it didn't look like Mr. Pullman anymore, but her Uncle Jason.

"This is math," Jayla said and looked down at her test. She pressed her pencil onto the problems written on the paper to try and stop them from swirling. Just then, the tip of her pencil broke as the bell rang—so loud it woke Jayla up. She gazed at the ceiling above her bed and saw the few glow-in-the-dark stars that still clung to the plaster. They had long since dimmed from when she'd gone to bed for the night. Somewhere in the house, the phone rang again. It wasn't a school bell after all and she wasn't taking the world's most terrible math test. She was home, but it was late.

And someone was calling.

A light came on in the hallway, throwing a wide

beam of brightness into her room. A moment later, she saw her dad walk across the hardwood floor. The floor creaked under his bulky weight. The cordless phone half rang again before he picked it up.

"Hello?" she heard her dad mumble.

Jayla sat up in her bed, wondering who would be calling so late. She looked at her alarm clock. It was 1:13 a.m. She didn't like late night or early morning calls. The last time the phone range this late, she remembered getting bad news.

She tried to figure out who her dad was talking to but couldn't determine it from his end of the conversation. He nodded and said "okay" a bunch of times, but not much else.

Her little brother, Dion, walked into the hallway too. He rubbed his sleepy eyes and tugged on her dad's pajama pant bottoms.

"Who is it, Dad?" Dion asked, following the question up with a yawn big enough to swallow his face.

Her dad put up a just-a-minute finger and put the phone to his other ear.

"So, tomorrow morning? First thing?" he asked.

The person on the other end must have said the right thing. Her dad nodded.

"Will do," he said. "Thanks for the call."

As her dad hung up the phone, Jayla swung out of bed. She kicked her slippers out of the way instead of putting them on and joined the rest of her family.

"Who was that?" Jayla asked.

"It was Jerry at the office," her dad said. "Sorry his call woke you guys up."

Dion looked toward the window above the stairs and stared out into the pitch-black sky.

"Why'd he call so late?" Dion asked.

"Early, you mean," Jayla corrected. "It's past one in the morning."

"Whoa," Dion said. "That's late—I mean, early!"

"We're going to go on a spring break trip," Dad said. "And we're leaving first thing tomorrow morning."

Jayla started to think she was still dreaming. They hadn't gone on a vacation in years, not since their mom had left and Grandma had died.

"It's only Thursday morning. Spring break doesn't start until next week. And where are we going, anyway?" Jayla asked, likely beating her little brother's same question by a breath.

"Colorado," her dad said. "Some of the trails in the Rocky Mountain National Park got washed out and they want a crew out there right away to fix them." Then he added, "I guess we'll just have to start spring break a little early this year."

Jayla wondered why that was such an emergency. Was there such a huge rush to fix trails that they needed to call and wake everyone? And they had to leave tomorrow?

"Is that the state with all the mountains?" Dion asked.

"Yeah, buddy," Dad said. "The Rocky Mountains. We'll be staying in a little town called Estes Park. It's in Colorado and the base for the park."

"I need to get online and find us plane tickets," her dad said, walking into his room.

Jayla and Dion followed. Dad picked his laptop up off the dresser and pressed the power button. As he walked by the bed, he tossed the laptop down and went into the closet for a suitcase.

"Are we going to have to work too?" Dion asked.

"If you have any homework, yes," Dad said. "Actual landscaping? No. Leave that to me and the crew they put together, okay, D?"

Dion nodded. Jayla sighed. She knew her little brother didn't have much in the way of homework, being in second grade. But seventh graders? They always had plenty to do.

Especially math.

At least we're not going on a vacation in the middle of the school year, Jayla thought. I'd never catch up.

"Are you going to let school know I'll be missing a couple days?" Jayla asked.

"First thing in the morning," Dad replied. "It shouldn't be a big deal to miss a couple days before spring break anyway, I'm sure."

"How long will we be gone?" Jayla asked.

"Jerry says we're guaranteed a week," Dad said, throwing some undershirts and socks into his suitcase. "Could be more, I suppose."

It was easy to see her dad was excited about the trip. Working for a landscaping company in Chicago meant a lot less work during the winter. In the off-season, her dad had to plow parking lots for businesses and the driveways of some homeowners.

"Do you want to know the best part?" Dad asked, turning his attention to his laptop. He opened a travel website to look for plane tickets. "The company pays for everything. Even having you guys come along. They really need me out there."

Jayla and Dion looked at each other. It was hard to be too upset about missing school. And it wasn't every day they got to go on a plane and fly to Colorado.

After twenty minutes or so, all the arrangements were made. Their flight was at 6:10 a.m. to Denver. In the meantime, Jayla had to pack.

She grabbed four pairs of jeans, a few tops, and plenty of warm socks. She looked at her school backpack and kicked it. The thought of bringing her math book on a trip didn't seem fair, or right. After packing her toothbrush and mouthwash, she came back to her bag.

"Fine," she said, unzipping the backpack. "But you're not going to ruin this trip for me."

Jayla tugged the thick textbook out and saw the worksheet that was due on Friday. It was folded in half and sticking out from the middle of the book. It didn't look like that one was getting to Mr. Pullman on time.

In the hallway, she saw Dion struggling with his bag. It looked like he had a load of bricks in it.

"This is too heavy," Dion groaned.

Jayla came out to help her little brother. She grabbed the bag and lifted it. Her arms strained under the weight.

"I don't think the plane will take off with this bag on board," she joked. "What do you have in here?"

"All of my books," Dion announced, proudly.

Jayla unzipped his bag and looked inside. Dion

wasn't lying. Just about every single book the kid owned was stuffed inside.

"You can't bring all of these," Jayla said. "Did you even pack any clothes?"

"No," Dion said. He pointed to the jeans and hooded sweatshirt he was wearing. "I'll just wear these all week."

"Oh, no you won't," she said. "After a day, you'll start to stink."

"You'll stink," Dion snapped.

"Boys always smell worse than girls," Jayla said. "That's just science."

Jayla helped him pick out the five books he couldn't live without and stuffed some clothes inside there too. In no time, he was able to sling the bag over his shoulder.

"Nice," he said.

Before long, they had their bags lined up by the front door, ready to go. Her dad told them both to get back into bed and try to get a few more hours of sleep. They'd need to be up early to get to the airport.

Jayla hopped into bed, wider awake than ever. She watched as the stars above her bed slowly lost their glow. Once the rest of the house was quiet, Jayla heard footsteps in the hallway. A moment later, there was a shadow across her doorway.

"Who is it?" Jayla asked, trying her hardest not to sound scared.

"It's me," the Dion-shaped shadow said. "I can't sleep."

Jayla sighed. "Neither can I."

"Can I come lay with you?"

"Sure," Jayla said. "But keep quiet."

"Okay," Dion replied, and ran to the left side of her bed. He hopped in and pulled the covers over him. Both of them lay in silence, staring up at the ceiling stars.

"It's going to feel weird," Dion said suddenly.

"What do you mean?" Jayla asked. "Going to Colorado? They say the air up in the mountains is—"

"No," Dion said, cutting her off. "It's going to feel weird going on a trip without Mom."

Jayla shifted in the bed. She'd thought the same thing but had planned to keep it to herself. The less she thought about Mom, the better. After all, she was the one who left the three of them.

"Yeah," Jayla said finally. "But she probably wouldn't like it up in the mountains anyway."

"Why not?" Dion asked. She could feel him scratching his leg under the blankets.

"She's afraid of heights," Jayla said. "We'll be way above sea level."

Dion was quiet for a moment and then spoke up.

"You're making that up, aren't you?" he said. "About Mom being scared."

"I might be," Jayla said. "Now shut up. We're supposed to be sleeping."

The two of them were quiet, and before too long, Jayla was asleep. This time around, she didn't dream about Mr. Pullman's impossible math class. Instead, she dreamed of mountains, snow, and airplanes.

What seemed like ten minutes later, a voice broke through her dream.

"Time to go to Colorado, guys," Dad said, almost sounding excited. "The mountains are waiting for us!"

CHAPTER 2

A HOTEL NAMED STANLEY

By the middle of the next day, Jayla Walters was in love. While she liked living in Chicago and considered herself a city girl, she loved Colorado and thought it was beautiful.

The scenery kept unspooling in front of them as they drove their windy way into the mountains. There were clusters of rock formations on the hills, deep valleys, and streams running alongside the road. Dion was pressed up against the window, "oohing" and "ahhing" at the Rocky Mountain views. He'd even put down the book that he'd started reading back in Denver.

That was saying something, Jayla thought.

"This is beautiful," Dad said. "Just breathtaking, isn't it?"

"Is that because of the air up here, Dad?" Dion asked.

"What do you mean, D?" he asked.

"Breathtaking," Dion said. "Because the air isn't so fat up here?"

"The air is thinner," Jayla said. "But that's because we're at a higher elevation. We're like seven thousand feet above sea level."

She'd been watching their progress on her smartphone's map, following their car's dot as they wound through the mountains. At times, the dot would stall when the internet wasn't so great, but it soon caught up. On another page, she did as much research as she could on the town of Estes Park.

Unlike Chicago, there wasn't a whole lot there.

"How come we didn't stay in Denver?" Jayla asked.

"Because it's an hour and a half each way," Dad said. "And since you guys will be on your own during the day, I wanted us to be close."

That was one of the big drawbacks about their trip. Jayla and Dion were going to be stuck alone together for long chunks of time while their dad was working during the day. Sure, she would be finishing the remainder of her homework, which was due before spring break officially started, to pass some of the time, but the bulk of it would be spent with Dion.

"That makes sense," Jayla said. "I just wonder if

we're going to go crazy after a few days, being stuck at the hotel."

"Is there a pool?" Dion asked, finally turning away from the window.

"There is . . ." Dad said slowly.

"Yes!" Dion shouted. "This is going to be—"

"But it's outside," Dad continued, before Dion could finish. "And it'll be too cold for it to be open."

"It could be open," Dion said, hopefully.

"It's March," Jayla said. "There's no way."

"It could be," Dion said quietly.

After a while, they drove down a curving hill and a small town became visible. The road ahead of them curled away from a lake, leading into a small downtown area.

Jayla looked to the right and saw a road sign that signaled they were in Estes Park.

"We're here," she said.

As they drove through town, Jayla studied the surroundings of where they'd be staying for the next week. It looked just like any other small town, except that it sat in what seemed like a bowl with mountains all around it. The buildings were short and kind of plain. They weren't any taller than a few stories. It was nothing like downtown Chicago with its soaring skyscrapers.

"Where are we staying?" Dion asked.

Dad looked off toward the right, squinting a little. "You'll see it when we get a little closer," he said. "It really stands out."

Oh great, Jayla thought. It's going to be some sort of huge dump.

Both she and Dion started looking for it among the small businesses, trying to see if they could find what their dad was talking about. There were a bunch of different accommodations, and any time Dion saw the word "hotel" or "motel," he called them out.

"Is it that one, Dad?" Dion asked.

"Nope," Dad replied. "Keep looking."

Jayla scanned the horizon. No hotels she saw stood out to her. As they rounded a corner and headed up a hill, she saw a place that looked magnificent. It was a gigantic mansion.

"Are we staying at The Stanley Hotel?" Jayla asked, spotting the huge sign along the side of the road.

"And the girl wins a new car," Dad said. "But not really, because you're not old enough to drive."

Dion laughed and their dad smiled at them through the rearview mirror.

"You like that one?" he asked.

"The hotel is named Stanley?" Dion asked. "What was wrong with Hotel Herbert or Louise Lodge?"

"Very funny, D," Dad said, as they pulled up. "This place was built by a guy who helped invent steam engine cars. They called them Stanley Steamers, I think."

"This place is huge," Jayla said, still marveling at the hotel.

The Stanley Hotel was a grand white structure, with white pillars and a large upper balcony above the entrance. There were tons of windows and a small spire with a flag on top of it. The roof was red and had a few peaks with windows that looked out onto the town.

It didn't look like a hotel at all. It looked like a billionaire's mansion.

"We're really staying here?" Dion asked, sounding a little confused.

"Yeah," Dad said. "Pretty cool, isn't it?"

"This big of a place and they don't have an indoor pool?" Dion said unsatisfied. "Couldn't we stay somewhere else?"

Dad sighed as he parked the rental car near the front.

"I tried," Dad said. "But everything else is booked.

So, the Walters crew gets to stay in the fanciest hotel in town."

"More like the United States," Jayla said. "This place is insane."

"Oh, there are fancier places," Dad said, turning off the engine. "In New York, Las Vegas, places like that. If they ever get a lot of storms and need emergency landscaping done, maybe we'll stay there. But for now? The Stanley is our home for the week."

"What's up, Stanley?" Dion said, laughing at his own joke.

Oh boy, Jayla thought. *It's going to be a long week with this kid.*

———

As impressed as Jayla was with the outside of the hotel, the inside blew her away.

"This is the fanciest place I've ever seen in my life," Dion whispered, clutching his book to his chest.

Jayla walked slowly around the lobby as their dad went to the front desk to get them checked in. Carved, ornate arches framed the doorways. The sun shone through front windows on beautiful hardwood floors. A carpeted staircase that branched into two separate sets of steps stood next to the check-in desk.

"Check out these chairs," Dion said, plopping down on a plush leather chair.

"Dion," Jayla whispered. "I don't think you're supposed to sit on those."

"Why are you whispering?" Dion said. "We're not in a library."

He's right, Jayla realized. There was something about the place that made her feel like she had to be quiet. She couldn't explain it. Jayla wondered if it was because she felt like she didn't belong there. Her family wasn't fancy at all. It felt weird to be in a place as nice as The Stanley Hotel.

"Just be careful," Jayla said. "Everything just seems really old."

An older man and woman laughed to themselves as they walked over to the windows to look out over Estes Park. The floor creaked under their feet as they walked.

"Okay, guys," Dad said as he headed their way. "We're all set. Got the last room in the place. We're in Room 217."

Though there weren't a lot of people in the lobby, they all seemed to go quiet at the same time. Jayla saw the man and woman at the window whisper to each other. The man looked over his shoulder at them and raised his eyebrows.

"You're in for an interesting night," the man said with a chuckle. His wife smacked his shoulder.

"Howard," she blurted. "Stop that."

And just like that, the two of them walked away. Jayla looked at her brother and dad, but neither of them seemed to notice. They were too busy messing with their suitcases.

"Let's go, Jay," Dion said.

Jayla nodded and looked around the lobby again before following her family to the fancy staircase. The wheels on her luggage made light clicking sounds on the hardwood floor.

Interesting night? What did those old people mean?

———

At the end of the hallway was Room 217. Their dad inserted the key and the electronic mechanism turned the light on the door handle green. It unlocked with a *click*. A moment later, her dad swung the door open. At first glance, Jayla knew it was going to be trouble.

"Dad," Dion whined, walking into the room and letting his suitcase fall to the floor. "There's only one bed."

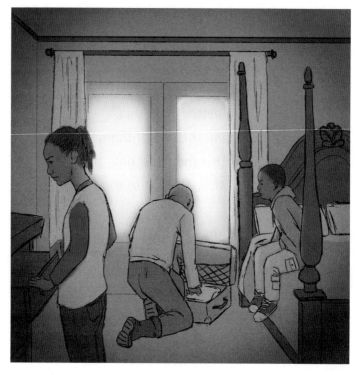

"Yeah, about that," Dad began wheeling his own bag to the side of the bed. "We're going to have to make do."

"Seriously, Dad?" Jayla asked, shaking her head. "You don't expect us all to sleep in one bed, do you?"

"No, no," Dad said.

"Because he makes noises in his sleep," Jayla continued, not hearing him. "It's like sleeping near a wild animal."

"I do not!" Dion shouted. "At least I don't fart in my sleep!"

"What?" Jayla cried.

"Hey, hey," Dad said, raising his voice. "That's enough of that! We're not going to cram all three of us in the bed. There's no way that's going to fly. The front desk is going to bring a cot for me to sleep in."

"Can't we just stay somewhere else?" Jayla asked. "I don't know why, but this old place kind of gives me the creeps. It's just so fancy and . . ." her voice trailed off as she looked around the ornate room.

"This is it," Dad said. "Last place in town, so we have to make it work. You two have the nice bed, so learn how to get along."

Jayla wanted to say more, but kept her mouth shut. The trip wasn't ideal, but she owed it to her dad to at least try and make things work. She moved her suitcase to the side of the room where there was a small fabric-covered chair in the corner.

Dion went to use the bathroom while her dad sat on the edge of the bed to check a text message. Jayla sat on the chair and kicked off her shoes. The bed had huge posts on every corner, there was a flat-screen TV on one of the dressers, and small tables were placed on each side of the bed. The table legs looked like they could've come off a wooden dog.

Jayla stood up and turned to look out the window. She could see bits of the red roof of the hotel through melted patches in the snow. She scanned the beautiful snow-topped mountains surrounding the small town. She wondered where her dad was going to have to work to help fix the trails.

"Early start tomorrow," Dad said. Jayla turned to see him shaking his head at his phone. "I guess I shouldn't complain. Work is work, right?"

"Definitely," Jayla said. She looked down to the floor. A chill raced up her back.

Where were her shoes? To her surprise, they were no longer on the floor by the chair but placed neatly against the wall near the bathroom door.

A moment later, the toilet flushed and Dion came out, wiping his hands on his jeans.

"What happened to you, Jay?" he asked, staring at his older sister.

Jayla didn't say anything, but instead looked over to her dad, still texting with whoever was in charge of the landscaping work he needed to do.

Neither of them could have moved my shoes, Jayla

thought, feeling her heart thump a little harder in her ribs. *And if they didn't, and I didn't . . . then who did?*

"Okay," Dad said, snapping Jayla out of her thoughts. "Let's figure out the food situation in this town. Who's hungry?"

Dion answered quickly and Jayla grabbed her shoes. She was suddenly very eager to get out of that room.

CHAPTER 3

THE VISITOR

For dinner that night, the Walters stopped at a place near their hotel for New York–style pizza.

"What's wrong with Colorado-style pizza?" Dion asked.

"I don't think there is such a thing," Jayla replied, looking over the top of her menu at her brother.

"There is," Dad said. "But it's got little bits of rock and pine needles in it."

Dion set his menu down for a moment and looked at his dad. "Are you serious?"

Dad shrugged and pretended to look at the menu some more, while Jayla shook her head and laughed.

"He's messing with you," she said. "Like Colorado-style means they put bits of the mountain and pine cones in every slice."

"Yeah, no thanks," Dion said. "I like extra cheese, hold the gravel."

When dinner was over, the three of them headed

across the parking lot toward their rental car. It was already dark, even though it was early in the evening.

"Do we have to go back?" Jayla asked as she climbed in. She could see The Stanley Hotel up on the hill. The front of the building was lit up, giving it an eerie, yellow glow.

"You don't like the hotel?" Dad asked. "It's really the nicest place in town."

Jayla had to think about what to say. She couldn't tell them that her shoes had mysteriously moved across the room on their own. Her dad would think she's losing her mind. Even worse, it would probably scare Dion.

"We're just going to be stuck in the hotel for the week," Jayla said. "It'd be nice to stay out as long as we can."

"I know," Dad said, buckling his seatbelt. "But we didn't get much sleep last night and I've got an early morning tomorrow. I need to get as much rest as I can."

"I'm pretty worn out too, Dad," Dion said.

"It's been a big day for all of us," Dad said as he started the car. "We could all use some shut-eye."

"Okay," Jayla agreed. She took a deep breath. *Let's hope I can actually rest in that place*, she thought.

Around 10:30 p.m., everyone but Jayla was asleep in Room 217. She had the lamp beside the bed on, hoping that would help keep her from getting creeped out. Dion shifted on his side of the bed a little and grumbled.

"Can you turn that light off?" he whispered, half awake.

Jayla looked around the room one last time. Her dad was sleeping on the little cot off to the right, near Dion's side of the bed. The bathroom door was closed and it didn't seem like there was anything strange about the room.

She reached over and turned off the light. As her eyes adjusted to the darkness, she lay very still and listened. There were only the sounds of her dad lightly snoring and the occasional creak of his cot.

There's nothing to be afraid of, Jayla thought. *Maybe Dion moved the shoes. Maybe I did and just didn't remember.*

Jayla told herself that over and over until her eyes got heavy. She glanced at the closed bathroom door one more time before her eyes slipped shut and she fell asleep.

———————

Cold.

Despite having a pretty heavy comforter on the bed, Jayla was cold. She opened her eyes, fairly certain that her little brother had rolled himself up in the thick blanket. A second later, she realized that wasn't the case. She had plenty of covers on her side of the bed.

The *room* was cold.

Jayla sat up slightly and nearly shrieked at what she saw.

There was a woman in their room.

Before Jayla could move or make a sound, the woman walked toward her side of the bed until she was standing almost next to her. Waves of cold and terror washed over Jayla as she slipped her face under the covers. She considered covering herself completely to hide, but couldn't. Something inside her told her that she needed to watch this woman.

She's a ghost, Jayla thought. *There's a ghost in our room!*

Everything in her wanted to throw the light on and scream to wake her dad and brother up, but she couldn't. Though she'd never been paralyzed and didn't know exactly what that was like, that's how she felt. She was stuck.

As her pounding heart threatened to burst, Jayla noticed something different about the lady. Jayla could see right through her to the door on the other side of the room. Even so, she could make out the clothes the lady was wearing. It looked like an old-time maid's uniform. She wore a dark long-sleeved dress with white straps that connected to an apron around her waist. On top of her head was a white bonnet-like hat.

The maid didn't look at Jayla, which made it a little easier for her to watch the mysterious visitor, but not much. Even though the figure didn't seem to want to harm her, Jayla was afraid to look away. The woman's dark eyes looked ahead to the wall next to the bed, and Jayla could make out some of the details in her face. She was a younger lady, probably in her mid-twenties. Her eyes seemed empty and her mouth held tight as if she was concentrating on something.

Please don't hurt us, Jayla thought, shivering under her heavy blankets.

She watched as the maid reached her hand up to the wall, holding it there a moment. The maid then turned and walked back toward the door to the hallway, but paused halfway in between. She crouched down and Jayla held her breath.

She's going under the bed, she thought. *The ghost is going to hide under the bed and get us when I'm asleep again.*

Before Jayla could even think to scream, the maid stood up again. She brushed her skirt straight with her hands and walked out, passing through the closed door.

The room was silent and still. Jayla exhaled, realizing how long she'd held her breath. After a moment, the chill in the air dissipated and it seemed like the world, at least the world inside of Room 217, went back to normal.

Dion grunted a little and flipped over to his side. Her dad's soft snores drifted through the darkness. Jayla was pretty sure she could hear her heart rapidly drum the inside of her ribcage.

She lay there motionless, afraid to move or do anything short of breathing. What would happen if she got up? If she woke up her dad to let him know what she'd seen, would the ghostly maid come back? Could she hurt them somehow?

I hate this place, Jayla decided. She'd had an uneasy feeling about the hotel before, but just then, she realized why. It was haunted and they were stuck there for the whole week.

At night, Dion sometimes liked to climb into bed with her when he was scared. Suddenly, she knew how he felt. Jayla was tempted to wake him up so that she didn't feel so frightened and alone.

I can't do that, Jayla realized. *He's going to be even more scared if I tell him what I've seen. He'll never be able to get to sleep and he'll be a nightmare to watch tomorrow when Dad's at work. I need to pull it together and be brave. That's all there is to it.*

Jayla looked over to where the ghost had passed through the closed door and into the hallway. There didn't seem to be any sign of the paranormal visitor, and the room didn't feel as chilly as it had before. She just hoped that meant the ghost was gone for good.

Wanting to prove to herself that she wasn't scared, Jayla pulled the covers aside for a moment. Taking a deep breath, she swung her legs out from under the covers and placed her bare feet on the floor. The carpet felt soft and warm, as if the room had not been icy cold only moments before.

Maybe I just dreamed the whole thing, Jayla thought. *Or maybe at age twelve, I'm already starting to go a little crazy!*

She stood up and walked toward the bathroom door.

It was still closed and she was thankful for that. If it was open and dark inside, just about anything could jump out at her without warning. If something opened the door, at least she'd have a second to turn and run.

But the ghost didn't open the door, Jayla reminded herself.

She shook her head slightly, trying to knock the dumb thoughts from her head. Jayla reminded herself to be brave, not talk herself into being terrified by something she might or might not have seen.

With new determination, Jayla walked slowly along the side of the bed. When she reached the end, she put her hand on the thick wooden bedpost. She stopped to listen for any weird noises, but the room was mostly silent.

Jayla decided what she would do. She'd look out into the hallway to see if the ghost was out there. Though she wasn't sure what she'd do if she *did* see the spooky maid, at least she'd be able to know whether she was just seeing things.

As she took another step past the little bench at the end of the bed, the floor beneath her feet creaked. It took everything in her to not shriek, dive back under the covers, and never come out again.

Instead, she exhaled nice and slow and closed her eyes for a moment. The room didn't get cold again, and she didn't feel that strange tingle down her back. Other than her brother and dad, she was alone and nothing was happening.

Jayla opened her eyes and let them readjust to the little bit of light coming through the window. She continued to the door and paused. She hadn't noticed before, but their room didn't have a peephole to look out into the hallway. They usually made everything look distorted, as if peering through a fish-eye lens.

If she wanted to look outside, she'd have to open the door.

I have to know, Jayla decided. *Even if it might wake up Dion and Dad.*

She reached down and undid the lock, trying as carefully as she could to be quiet. It released with a soft *thunk* and she turned the knob. Jayla could only pray that there wouldn't be a spooky face waiting for her on the other side.

Slowly, she opened the door, letting a tiny sliver of light into their room. She squinted from the lights in the hallway.

When she had the door cracked a few inches and

her eyes had adjusted, Jayla found that the hallway was empty. The fancy patterned carpet stretched down the hallway, past the other rooms.

Nothing here, Jayla thought, keeping the door open a moment or two longer. If there had been a ghost in her room, she didn't see it in the hallway. She wondered if it went and visited the other rooms. Maybe there were other people staying in the hotel, scared and shivering in their beds too.

"Okay," Jayla whispered. "Then stay out."

She slowly closed the door, darkening the room again. Being extra careful, she locked the door, knowing locks didn't do anything to keep ghosts away. Jayla turned and saw that the rest of her family was still asleep. As carefully as possible, she walked backward, keeping her eye on the door until she reached her side of the bed.

Hoping she wouldn't stir Dion, she slipped back under the covers.

Maybe I just dreamed the whole thing, Jayla said to herself again. As she settled into her pillow and stared up at the ceiling, she felt a small hand touch her arm.

"Is she gone?" Dion's voice was barely audible.

Jayla flinched. She wasn't sure if her little brother was talking in his sleep or what was going on.

"What?" Jayla whispered. "What are you talking about?"

Dion sat up and opened his eyes wide. "The hotel lady," he whispered back. "I saw her too."

CHAPTER 4

CREEPY CAVES

Jayla woke up the next morning with a start. She was stunned that she and her brother were able to fall asleep at all after what they'd seen. Jayla looked at the time on her phone and saw that it was almost 9 a.m.

"Wake up, D," Jayla whispered. She grabbed his shoulder and rocked him back and forth.

"I'm still so tired," Dion groaned and rolled to his side.

Jayla nodded. She was tired too, and couldn't remember what time they'd fallen asleep. As much as she wanted to talk with Dion about the ghost lady last night, they decided they couldn't risk waking up Dad. Before they went to bed, Dad had complained more than a few times that he was going to have a very early morning.

After a few more groans about being tired, Dion sat up and squinted at the room door.

"Dad left a note," Dion said, sleepily.

He climbed out of bed and pulled a piece of Stanley Hotel stationery off the door. Using the sitting bench at the end of the bed as a springboard, he launched himself back onto the covers.

"What's it say?" Jayla asked. She still looked around the room, worried that their visitor might decide to make her rounds early.

"Good morning, guys," Dion read. "I didn't want to wake you since I was up before just about everyone else in Estes Park. Go ahead and order some breakfast and lunch. I should be back by dinnertime. I could go for that pizza again."

"That pizza was pretty good," Jayla admitted.

Dion nodded. "Yeah, I liked it too."

"What else did he say?" Jayla asked.

"Oh, right," Dion said, then picked up where he left off. "Try to stay out of trouble when I'm gone and MOST IMPORTANTLY . . ."

Dion help up the note. "He capitalized that part."

"Of course he did," Jayla said and smiled.

"Behave yourselves and get along. Love, Dad," Dion finished. He flipped the paper over to see if there was anything else written on the other side.

"I was hoping to tell him our room was haunted," Jayla said. "Then maybe we could get out of here."

A silence passed between them. The room was quiet,

as if the word "haunted" made it true. Dion set the note from Dad aside and hugged himself. His brown eyes darted around Room 217 as if he meant to make sure it was safe for them to talk.

"So what was that?" Dion asked quietly. "Who was that lady?"

Jayla shrugged. "I have no idea," she said. She looked again to the door leading out into the hallway. "And I was trying to tell myself it was just a dream until you said you saw her too."

Dion shivered, thinking back to the night before.

"I woke up because I was really cold. I was going to get up and grab a blanket, but when I saw that lady, I thought *forget it*. I just pretended to be asleep," Dion said, eyes wide. "I thought maybe if I didn't move or look like I was awake, she'd leave us alone. It worked."

Jayla stood up and walked over to where the ghost had stopped at the wall along her side of the bed. There was nothing there that she could see. Just a painted wall.

"She stopped and touched the wall here," Jayla said. "I'm not sure why."

Dion twisted up his mouth before responding. "I don't know what she was doing and I don't want to know. I'm just glad she didn't try to get us."

Jayla walked over to the long dresser beneath the TV and picked up the hotel's menu. There were all sorts of fancy breakfasts that they could order and have delivered to their room.

"Do you want to eat in here or downstairs?" Jayla asked.

"What do you think?" Dion said.

"Downstairs," they both said together.

Jayla and Dion took showers, then got themselves dressed and ready to go. Jayla had to remind Dion that wearing pajama pants someplace as fancy as The Stanley wasn't a good idea. She was pretty sure people would give him strange looks and they didn't want to be "those" kids.

After they were seated in the restaurant, Jayla looked around. They were the only kids there. The other customers were older than them by at least thirty years. The older couple they'd seen in the lobby the day before was there too, eating omelets. Seeing them reminded Jayla of what the old guy said when he heard they were staying in Room 217.

You're in for an interesting night.

"I didn't think ghosts were real," Dion said before

taking a sip of his orange juice. It was in a goblet-like glass and he held it like he was some sort of king toasting his royal subjects.

"Neither did I," Jayla said. "Mom and Dad always told us that there were no such things as ghosts. After last night, I'm beginning to think they don't know what they're talking about."

"Well, that lady wasn't like the ghosts from movies and stuff," Dion said.

"You weren't scared?"

"Of course I was scared," Dion replied, taking another sip. "But she didn't seem like she was going to hurt us or anything."

Jayla hadn't thought of that. The ghost maid really didn't do anything besides make the room cold and startle both of them. But still, seeing the ghost of some strange woman was enough to make anyone nervous.

"Still," Jayla said. "We have to tell Dad."

"Yeah. He can tell the front desk that the room is haunted," Dion said. "People should know what kind of hotel this is."

That gave Jayla an idea. She pulled out her phone and typed in *Stanley Hotel*. There were a few hits that described where the hotel was and some information about booking a room. A little farther below that, Jayla found what she was looking for.

"Well," Jayla said. "Looks like a lot of people DO know what kind of hotel The Stanley is."

She turned her phone so that Dion could see some of the entries she found.

"What?" Dion said. "People know this place is haunted and they actually want to stay here?" Dion looked unconvinced.

"I guess so," Jayla said. "I don't think complaining about the ghostly maid is going to do any good."

A moment later, their breakfast arrived and they stopped talking about ghosts for a good twenty minutes.

———

Neither Dion nor Jayla were excited about going back to their room after breakfast. Even without the threat of the maid coming back to scare them, staying in the same room for hours until their dad came back just didn't sound like much fun.

"I really wish they had an indoor pool," Dion said as they walked out of the restaurant and toward the lobby.

Jayla and her brother made their way toward the staircase leading up to the second floor and continued on to the area behind it where there was a hallway.

They kept going down the hall until they reached a small museum-like room. There, on display, were old guest books, framed black-and-white photographs, and clothing from the early 1900s.

On one mannequin, an outfit caught Jayla's eye. It was a maid's uniform and looked exactly like the one the ghostly woman had been wearing the night before. Just seeing the white apron and the long black sleeves made the hairs on her arm stand up. Jayla stared at the faceless figure wearing the clothes. She took her phone out of her pocket and took a picture of it.

"Whoa," she whispered. "Dion, you need to see this."

There was no answer.

"D?" Jayla called, looking around the small museum. There was a group of people standing by a counter, waiting for a tour. Her brother wasn't there. She walked back out into the hallway and looked to the left and right. Dion was nowhere to be found.

Great, she thought, her thoughts spinning out of control. *Now he's lost in this giant-sized haunted house. Dad's going to flip out!*

"I'm right here," a voice whispered to her left. Jayla turned and found her brother, sitting on a bench in the hallway, his head in an ancient-looking book.

"I don't think you're supposed to be reading that," Jayla said. "It's probably just for decoration."

"Really?" Dion said, looking at the spine of the book. "It's about The Stanley. Did you know there are supposed to be tunnels underneath the hotel?"

"Really?" Jayla asked. "Where are they?"

"There's supposed to be a door in the hallway behind the front desk," Dion said, nodding to Jayla's right. "So, probably like . . ."

"Right here?" Jayla turned to see a door partially cracked open. Letting curiosity take over, she opened it slightly. Immediately, her heart sped up as fear tickled her neck and spine once again. She waited for the inevitable cold feeling to wash over her. A moment later, Dion's head peeked under her arm.

"Whoa," Jayla whispered. "Check this out!"

Before Dion could object and demand she get out of there, Jayla opened the door a bit wider. She looked around to see if the hotel management would catch them before she grabbed her little brother and dragged him inside with her.

"What are you doing?" Dion whispered as loud as he could without yelling. "We're not supposed to be . . ."

Dion's voice faded off as he took in their surroundings.

They were standing at the top of a wooden staircase that led down into what looked like a dark tunnel. The walls of the tunnel were chiseled out of stone, almost like it was a cave.

"You think those are the tunnels?" Jayla asked, pointing down the staircase.

"Yeah. They've got to be, right?" Dion said, slipping completely under her arm and taking in the view.

Jayla took another cautious step closer to the stairs and let the door creak shut behind her. The single light bulb at the top of the wooden stairs cast eerie shadows to the tunnels below.

"What are these tunnels for?" Jayla asked, not expecting an answer.

"Not sure," Dion said. "I didn't read that far."

Jayla took another look at the deep, dark black that hung like a mist a few steps down.

"We shouldn't go any further. We don't have a flashlight," Dion said. "Besides, we should—"

"I've got the flashlight on my phone," Jayla said.

"I don't think we should," Dion said. "We might get in trouble or something."

"So what? And seriously? You want to go back to our room?" Jayla asked. "Dad's not going to be back for hours."

Dion hesitated and that was all Jayla needed.

"We take a quick peek and then we get out before anyone even knows we're down there," Jayla said. "C'mon. We'll just be bored sitting in the room watching TV," Jayla shuddered, "or worse, doing math homework."

"Okay," he said. "But only for like five minutes, okay?"

Jayla swiped to the screen with the flashlight function. A small beam of light emitted from the back of her phone. She wondered if it would be enough to see through the darkness of the tunnels.

"Whoa!" Dion shouted, then covered his mouth when he realized he wasn't being sneaky enough. "Creepy."

The two of them descended into the darkness beneath the hotel. Jayla could feel her shoes scrape against loose rocks as she stepped onto an uneven floor. Like the walls, it felt like the floor was carved out of stone too.

They walked through the first passage and Jayla saw wires and pipes running along the ceiling. There were also heating ducts too. The light on her phone was tiny, but it was strong enough to give just enough light to see, around six inches in front of them. She turned around and realized she could no longer see the stairway where they'd come down.

"Let's go this way," Dion said, pointing to the right. "There's a passage that goes down a little deeper."

Jayla was a little nervous about going too far, but she was curious about what they would find.

They continued along the passageway. Along the path, there were open doorways that seemed somehow even more impossibly dark than the darkness around

them. At any moment, Jayla was sure a hand was going to reach out and grab them.

"This is pretty cool," Jayla admitted more to herself than her brother.

". . . *don't get lost,*" a voice she didn't recognize whispered.

Jayla stopped in her tracks. Dion's footsteps came to a halt too.

"What did you say?" Dion asked, his voice suddenly high with fear.

"I didn't say anything," Jayla whispered. "But I heard it too."

". . . *don't belong here.*" Again, there was a voice that didn't sound like anyone whom either of them recognized.

"Is there someone down here?" Jayla cried. "Hello?"

Just as she was about to suggest that they turn around and head back, Jayla saw the charge level on her phone go from eighty-eight percent to zero percent in a matter of seconds.

And just like that, she and Dion were standing in complete darkness.

CHAPTER 5

VOICE IN THE DARK

"What happened to your phone?" Dion asked, grabbing onto her left arm.

Even though Jayla could hear her brother right next to her, and feel him clinging to her, she couldn't see his face—or any other part of him. All she could see was the last thing her eyes had seen, her phone's screen, which left a rectangular impression of light on her eyes.

"The battery drained down to zero percent," Jayla whispered hoarsely. "It was like something pulled the charge right out of it."

She pushed the home button and the power button, but nothing happened. For a moment, the little image of a depleted battery lit up the space for a split second, then went dark again.

"We have to try and get out of here," Jayla told her brother, who was still gripping her arm so tightly that it was starting to tingle. She shook her arm to break free until he finally let go. "Let's retrace our steps back to the stairway."

Jayla turned around and put her hand out into the void, afraid of what she might touch. She brushed her fingers against chiseled stone. It was the wall of the tunnel. She turned again and bumped into Dion. She had no idea which way they needed to go.

"We're going to end up lost down here," Dion whispered. "But at least we haven't heard that creepy voice again."

Somewhere in the darkness, the faint sound of a child laughing echoed against the stone walls.

Jayla's stomach dropped. "That's even worse," she said.

"We need to find a way out of here. Now!" Jayla had seen a few horror movies and knew that creepy kids giggling in the dark was never a good sign.

"How?" Dion sounded panicked. "It's too dark!"

Somehow, her brother sounded farther away from her.

"Grab my vest," Jayla said. "We can't lose each other down here."

"I can't even see your vest!" Dion cried.

"Don't move," Jayla said. "Let me find you and we'll stay together so we don't get separated."

She reached out into the darkness, hoping that they wouldn't touch something gross like a dead body. After feeling around for a moment or two, she bumped into something. There was a cry of pain.

"Ow!" Dion shouted. "That was my eye!"

"Sorry," Jayla replied, then she felt his shoulder and then his arm. She grabbed him by the wrist and had him clutch her vest again. "Don't let go."

"This time I won't," Dion promised.

She felt along the walls, walking slowly forward, letting the wall lead them along the tunnel's hallway. Jayla wasn't sure they were going in the right direction, but knew it was better than standing there, waiting for something to get them. She just hoped they weren't headed deeper into the underground labyrinth.

"We see you," a young voice whispered farther off in the dark.

"Did you hear that?" Dion whispered, his voice high with panic.

Jayla nodded, but remembered her brother wouldn't be able to see her response.

"Yeah," she replied. "But let's pretend we didn't."

Jayla did her best not to breathe out more than she needed to. Somehow, in her head, she thought if she was quiet, the voices in the dark couldn't find the two of them. Dion wasn't nearly as quiet. He scraped his feet along the floor, making more noise than Jayla was comfortable with.

"You have to be quiet," Jayla said. "The whole hotel can hear you!"

"Maybe that's a good thing," Dion snapped back. "We might need help getting out of here! I knew this was a bad idea!"

After a few minutes of staggering through the blackness, Jayla's outstretched hand touched an old wooden door. "I found something," she cried.

"Shhhhhhh!" Dion shot back.

Tracing her hands along the wood, Jayla soon touched a rusty, wobbly doorknob. She didn't remember seeing anything like it in the tunnels when they'd had her phone light. A wave of panic washed over her. Small beads of sweat sprang up along her forehead.

"There's a door here," Jayla croaked.

"Open it," Dion replied. "It might be the way out."

"Or maybe there are dead things behind it," Jayla said quietly.

"Don't even say that," Dion said quickly. "Keep it closed, Jay."

Somewhere in the darkness, there was the sound of slow, careful footsteps.

"Are you moving?" Jayla asked.

"No," Dion whispered. "I'm too busy trying not to scream."

"Okay," Jayla said. "Don't. Don't move and don't make any noise. I think I hear something."

Jayla sucked in her breath and waited. Everything was completely still. She strained to hear something— anything. All was quiet until—

Footsteps again. Something was walking around in the dark with them.

And it was getting closer.

"I hear that," Dion whispered, practically in tears. "Someone is walking toward us. What are we going to do?"

Jayla touched the knob again. It could lead to an exit or it could open to something unpleasant. She thought of the ghost maid in their room and realized doors meant nothing to the supernatural.

"It's getting closer," Dion said again. He pressed himself up against his older sister until they were both mashed up against the rough carved wall of the dark tunnel.

Jayla listened to the sound. There was another footstep, then another. Each one was closer than the last. There was no way to deny it. Whatever was down there with them was getting closer with every step.

Just then, the doorknob started to rattle.

"Dion?" Jayla asked, in a frantic whisper. "Are you touching the doorknob?"

"No," Dion said. "I'm covering my eyes with my hands!"

"What?" she cried. "Why? It's already dark."

"I just am, okay?"

Jayla inched away from the door, guiding her brother with her. Something was on the other side of the door trying to come out and something else was coming their way. As much as she hated to admit it, it felt like they were trapped.

The knob continued to rattle as Jayla looked toward what she hoped was the other end of the hallway. A bright round light appeared in the dark, making her squint. She didn't know if it was a spirit orb like they sometimes showed on TV or something else entirely.

With her eyes adjusted to the dark, she couldn't see anything for a moment.

With every step, the light got closer and brighter. Jayla opened her mouth to scream, but Dion beat her to it. His small voice echoed through the dark passageways.

"Hey, hey," a kind, older voice called in the dark. "No need to shout, young man!"

Dion stopped and Jayla held onto his shoulders to protect him. She could feel her brother tremble with fear.

"Who's there?" Jayla called into the darkness. She was afraid of what the answer might be and even more afraid there would be no answer at all.

The light turned and illuminated an old face. It looked like a disembodied head, floating in the pitch black.

"Whoa," Dion cried. "What are you?"

"Oh, come on," the voice replied. "I know I'm not pretty, but I'm not that scary looking! I'm Reuben. I'm the head caretaker of The Stanley Hotel."

"You're not some sort of monster?" Dion asked. Jayla cringed as soon as he said it.

"Oh, no," Reuben replied. "I'm not anything of the sort. Just an old guy who helps take care of this place. But who, might I ask, are you?"

"I'm Jayla and this is my brother, Dion," she said. She didn't like to tell anyone too much about themselves but didn't feel like there was much choice. "We're visiting from Chicago with our dad."

Reuben moved the light away from his face a little, which made his big nose and deep wrinkles look less frightening.

"Nice to meet you two," Reuben said. He didn't seem upset that they were somewhere they shouldn't be, and not nearly as scary as anything they'd seen in the past day.

"Can you get us out of here?" Dion asked.

Reuben reached out his hand for Dion to take.

"That's why I'm here," Reuben said. "You two shouldn't be down here in the first place. Not unless you're on a tour."

"Okay," Jayla said. "Sorry. We didn't know."

"I tried to tell her," Dion said.

Jayla shot Dion an icy look.

Dion put his small hand in Reuben's. Jayla held onto her brother and let the old man guide them through the dark corridors, using only the beam of his flashlight to guide the way. In time, they reached the wooden staircase that they'd descended what felt like hours ago.

All three of them climbed up and exited into the bright hallway near where the tour groups gathered. An old black-and-white picture of the hotel hung on the wall next to them. In it, The Stanley looked old, empty, and foreboding. There were a few almost faceless figures walking around the front of the enormous hotel.

In the light, Jayla got a better look at the caretaker. He was wearing a dark green jumpsuit with his name embroidered over his left chest pocket. A worn leather tool belt hung around his waist. Reuben had a long beard, speckled with white and black hairs. He was mostly bald, except for the horseshoe of hair circling the back of his head. His bright brown eyes looked kind and wise, as if he knew plenty of things worth knowing.

"Thanks for your help," Jayla said. "We'd be down there the rest of the week if you hadn't come along."

"It's no problem," Reuben said. "And I'm sorry if I scared the two of you."

"Everything about this hotel is scary," Dion blurted. "Our room is haunted too."

"Is that right?" Reuben replied. "Are you in Room 217 by chance?"

Hearing their room number startled Jayla. She let out a small gasp.

The old guy just nodded and sighed. "Can you tell me what's happened in your room?" he asked.

"Well, okay," Jayla said. "Last night while we were sleeping, it got really cold, almost like someone left the window open. When I opened my eyes, I could see a woman walking toward me."

"Let me guess," Reuben said, sliding his flashlight into his utility belt. "The woman was wearing a maid's uniform? Like something out of the olden days?"

"Yes!" Dion cried. "That's exactly it. She was messing with the wall before she turned around and left, I think. That's what Jayla said, anyway. I didn't see it all because I hid under the blankets until she was gone."

Reuben nodded and scratched the side of his beard a few times.

"The Stanley Hotel has a history of ghosts and strange things happening," the caretaker replied. "People who love spooky stuff come from all over the world to try and see what the two of you have seen. There have been paranormal investigators from TV shows, writers, and even thrill seekers who just loved to try and scare themselves."

"Those people sound nuts," Dion said matter-of-factly.

"Maybe," Reuben said. "But it's been part of this hotel for a very long time. Something about this place draws the living and the dead to it."

Jayla shuddered. The idea that a hotel could draw ghosts and other creepy things to it made her blood turn cold. From the sounds of it, there was more than one ghost inhabiting the halls, rooms, and underground tunnels of The Stanley Hotel.

"We heard voices and laughing in the tunnels," Jayla said. "I wasn't sure if that was the ghost from our room following us or what was going on. I think it drained my phone so that we couldn't see anything."

"Yeah," Dion said. "And we found an old door somewhere down there. Whatever else was hanging out there in the darkness was laughing at us. It even made the doorknob we were standing next to rattle and shake like it wanted to get out."

Reuben shook his head knowingly as he closed the door to the tunnel.

"What was behind that door?" Jayla asked. "We thought about opening it, hoping it would lead us out of the tunnels."

"Just an old maintenance closet," Reuben said. "And I'm not sure what happened down there with the lights. I don't think any of the spirits meant to harm or scare you. I do know one thing though. I'm positive that whatever was down there with the two of you wasn't Elizabeth."

Jayla and Dion stood silent for a moment. "Who is Elizabeth?" Jayla finally managed.

"The ghost in Room 217," Reuben said. "Her name is Elizabeth."

CHAPTER 6

A MAID'S WORK IS NEVER DONE

"So the ghost has a name," Jayla whispered. "How do you know that?"

There was a squawking sound from Reuben's belt. He held up a finger before he reached behind and pulled a walkie-talkie from a clip behind his back.

"Go ahead, Jack," Reuben said and waited for a reply.

Jayla turned to her brother and saw that Dion's face was almost frozen in fascination. They weren't going crazy. There was a ghost in their room and she had a name. There were a million questions Jayla had for the old caretaker. If anyone knew the answers, it was Reuben!

"Okay," Reuben said into the mouthpiece. "I'll be there in a few."

"Hurry, man," Jack said on the other end. "Everything is getting wet."

The walkie-talkie had blue tape around the end of

the floppy antenna, and it looked like it had seen better days. Jayla watched as Reuben clipped it back onto his belt.

"I don't know what these guys are going to do when I retire," Reuben said. "You'd think something as simple as a burst pipe in the music hall was the end of the world or something."

The old guy turned to walk away, and Jayla saw her chance to get answers quickly slip out of her grasp.

"Just one more second, please," Jayla pleaded. "What can you tell me about Elizabeth?"

Reuben stopped for a moment, but she saw he was eager to get to where he was going. He looked down the hall, but turned back.

"Her name was Elizabeth Wilson and she was a maid here at the hotel back in the early 1900s," Reuben said. "There was a storm and an accident and she—"

"Are you on your way?" Jack cried through the walkie-talkie. "It's pretty bad, man!"

"Look," the caretaker said to Jayla and Dion. "I'm really sorry. I need to get over there to take care of this. I don't move as fast as I used to."

Reuben started to walk away, when Dion spoke up.

"Is Elizabeth going to hurt us?" he asked.

"Not a chance," Reuben replied. "She just does her thing and has never hurt a single soul."

Something about the way Reuben said "soul" made Jayla shudder. Before they could ask him anything else, he disappeared down the polished hallway, heading deeper into the hotel.

"Nice guy," Dion said, staring off down the corridor.

"Right, but could this place be any creepier?" Jayla replied.

She looked up at some of the old framed photographs on the wall. People from decades ago looked back at her with empty stares. Suddenly, every old-time face she saw seemed a little more frightening to her.

Was Elizabeth Wilson one of the faces in the pictures? Jayla wondered. She blinked and shook it off. There was no way she was going to let stories of ghosts and creepy tunnels get the better of her. Besides, Reuben said Elizabeth would never hurt a soul.

But would she hurt a living person? Before they were nothing more than a soul?

Jayla knew she was probably overthinking the whole thing. She sometimes took people way too literally.

"So what are we supposed to do?" Dion asked.

"For one thing, let's stay out of the tunnels," Jayla

TRAPPED IN ROOM 217

said, smacking her little brother on the shoulder. "I'm supposed to be taking care of you while Dad's working."

"Hey," Dion said. "The tunnels were your idea!"

Jayla shrugged and nodded. Being lost in the dark and scared out of her wits took a lot out of her. She wasn't sure what else they could do, so she thought it would be best if they headed back to the room.

"We should probably do our homework anyway," Jayla said.

"I don't have any homework," Dion said. "I'm seven."

"Then you can read one of your eight thousand books. Let's just stay out of trouble for a few hours," Jayla said. "Before anyone else finds out we were in those dumb tunnels."

———————

A few hours passed. Dion was stretched out on their dad's cot, reading *Adventures of Robot Randy,* while Jayla laid on their messed-up bed, struggling with her math homework. She'd been given her last test to correct and review. Her math teacher, Mr. Pullman, thought she could do better than a C-minus. Jayla wasn't so sure.

As she flipped over to the last page, Jayla groaned. It looked like nothing but red marks and a complete nightmare. She wasn't sure which was scarier, having

71

a ghost in her hotel room or knowing she had many more years of math homework ahead of her.

Feeling discouraged and distracted, Jayla picked up her freshly charged smartphone and opened up the web browser. She glanced over at Dion, who was lost in the little robot's adventures, and went back to her phone.

She typed "ghosts Stanley Hotel" into the search engine and waited for the two seconds it took to find something.

There were more than three hundred thousand results.

"Holy cow," Jayla whispered, scrolling down and reading the top several lines of the first few entries. There were pictures and stories, by people who had stayed at the hotel, posting about what they'd seen.

She opened some of the pictures and saw people with photo-flash-washed faces. Near them were little balls of light they called "orbs." Jayla squinted and zoomed in on the images, trying to see what the big deal was. She wasn't sure why they were so excited to see little colored circles on their photos.

You should see what I saw, Jayla thought, opening another link.

In the article was a picture of a bunch of people sitting around a window near some fancy-looking stairs.

There were a few blurry, smudge-like figures on the steps. One of them looked like a little girl watching the people.

"This place is infested," Jayla whispered.

"With bugs?" Dion asked, not taking his eyes off his book.

"No," Jayla replied. "Just . . . never mind."

Realizing she wasn't going to find what she was looking for, Jayla tried another search thread. This time she typed "Stanley Hotel Elizabeth Wilson."

What appeared made her gasp. The links that popped up mentioned the name that Reuben the caretaker had given them. They also contained their room number, 217. The old guy wasn't just messing around, trying to creep them out.

Is this the only room she haunts? Jayla wondered and quickly looked up from her phone.

She peered at the bathroom and the door leading out into the hallway. There was nothing weird about either of them, but she thought the moment she looked away, the ghostly maid might show up.

Almost afraid of what she'd find, Jayla opened the first article. There was a story about something that took place one night at the hotel in the early 1900s and what happened to Elizabeth. Though it was likely going to keep her awake all night, Jayla scrolled down and read the entire story, shaking her head the entire time. She couldn't believe what she was reading.

"What are you doing?" Dion asked. His copy of *Randy* was closed and his bookmark was in his hand.

It was the universal sign that her little brother had finished yet another one.

"I found out what happened to Elizabeth," Jayla said, wondering if she ought to say anything else.

"Tell me," Dion said. He tossed down his book and jumped onto the bed.

"Back in 1911, the power went out in the hotel," Jayla said.

"They had power back then?" Dion asked.

"I guess so," Jayla replied, but shook her head. "But be quiet so I can tell you."

"Fine, okay," Dion said.

"While all the rich people were downstairs eating and dancing and everything, they had maids come up and light the gas lamps that were in each of the rooms," Jayla said, skimming the article again. "They were there as a back-up in case the hotel lost power."

Dion was quiet, as instructed. Jayla could tell by looking at his face that he was preparing for the worst.

"So there was a gas leak in our room at the time that no one knew about. When Elizabeth came in with her candle to light the lamp, there was a huge explosion," Jayla explained.

"It killed her?" Dion asked, looking up at his sister. His eyes were unblinking and serious.

"Actually," Jayla said. "It didn't. The explosion blew her down to the first floor. She ended up in the dining room below our room."

"What?"

"Yeah, I know," Jayla said. "The explosion destroyed around ten percent of the hotel. But Elizabeth? She only ended up with two broken ankles and some minor burns."

"That's crazy," Dion said. "She must've been part superhero or something."

Jayla explained that Freelan Oscar Stanley, the owner and namesake of the hotel, paid for all her hospital bills, and when Elizabeth was healed up, she was made head chambermaid.

"Mr. Stanley told her she could have a job at the hotel for life. And she worked here pretty much until she died," Jayla said, reading the bottom of the article. "And they said that's when her ghost started to appear."

"Why is she still here?" Dion asked. "You think she really liked working at the hotel? I would've quit after getting blasted through a hole in the floor."

Jayla shrugged. It didn't make sense. She wasn't sure exactly what happened after you died, but she didn't think being trapped in Room 217 sounded right.

Why was Elizabeth still here?

She put her phone down and saw Dion staring off toward the bathroom door. He looked like he was in deep thought. Jayla started to worry that she'd completely traumatized the kid. He tilted his head and squinted.

"I don't remember hanging up our towels," he said suddenly.

"What are you talking about?" Jayla asked.

Dion pointed to the bathroom, then scrambled off the bed as if following his own finger.

"When we took showers this morning, we just threw the towels on the floor," Dion said.

Her brother walked into the bathroom and Jayla followed behind him. She looked around, and sure enough, the towels were nicely folded and hung back on the racks. Neither of them had done that, as they were used to throwing their towels into a hamper back home. They never thought to hang them back up.

"Easy," Jayla said. "The maid did it."

"Elizabeth?" Dion asked. "The ghost maid?"

"No," Jayla said, but then hesitated. "Probably the real housekeeping staff that works here now. Maybe they did it while we were in the tunnels this morning."

Dion shook his head.

"Then why didn't they make our bed?"

Jayla turned. The bed was just as messy as it had

been when they'd left earlier in the morning. If house-keeping had come in to tidy up the room, wouldn't they have made their bed too?

"I don't know," Jayla mumbled more to herself than her little brother. She remembered how her shoes had been straightened and lined up against the wall.

Had that been Elizabeth? Was she straightening their room for them by hanging the towels up? Did she not know that her job was done here at The Stanley Hotel?

"It's her, isn't it?" Dion asked. "She's doing her chores like she still works here. How creepy is that?"

Jayla went over and touched the towels. They were still damp from when they'd showered hours earlier, but they were nicely folded and hung as if they were fresh and clean, right off the housekeeping cart.

"I think you're right," Jayla admitted. "I think she straightened my shoes when we first got here too. I thought maybe I was going crazy."

Dion trembled in an overexaggerated shiver.

"I just got the chills," he said, hopping up and down in the middle of the bathroom. "And we've got to be here the rest of the week? This is bananas!"

As they headed out of the bathroom, there was a loud knock, inches from where they stood.

Both Jayla and Dion screamed.

CHAPTER 7

CAUGHT ON CAMERA

"Housekeeping," a voice from out in the hallway said. It took Jayla a moment to catch her breath and to slow her racing heartbeat down. After a second, she realized that the real maid was there to make their beds and hang new towels for them.

The other maid beat you to it, Jayla thought.

"Hi," Jayla called through the door. "Can you come back a little later?"

"Yes ma'am," the woman replied.

"I almost had a heart attack," Dion whispered, collapsing into an over-dramatic pile on the floor. "Dang."

Jayla let out a deep breath and nodded in agreement. They were getting a little too anxious about the whole ghost situation. And, based on what she found on the internet, they might very well be some of the only people on the planet who hadn't known The Stanley was haunted.

"We need to take it easy, I think," Jayla said. "Obviously, this Elizabeth isn't looking to hurt us."

"I think you're right," Dion said. "I think she just wants to tidy up the room a bit. I guess that's what housekeeping or chambermaids do, isn't it?"

"Yeah," Jayla said. "And maybe we're messier guests than she's used to."

Dion was quiet for a moment. Jayla could see her little brother was thinking something pretty deep by the way he was moving his mouth back and forth a bit.

"Still," he finally said. "I feel kind of bad for her."

"Why?" Jayla replied. "It sounded like she liked working here, even after the accident."

"Yeah, but she's stuck here," Dion said. "Like she can't go wherever she's supposed to next."

Jayla hadn't thought of it that way. Maybe there was something keeping Elizabeth connected to Room 217. Maybe she was haunting the room for some reason.

"I don't know," Dion said. "I wish we could help her move on or whatever."

Jayla thought about what she'd learned so far and everything that had happened since.

"Well," she said. "Maybe we can."

———

They spent the rest of the afternoon in the room, watching TV and doing homework. When their dad finally came back, he looked exhausted and dirty from working in the mud and sludge all day.

"Those trails are so messed up," he said. "I'm not sure how we're going to get it all done in a week."

Jayla and Dion looked at each other and raised their eyebrows at the same time. Neither of them seemed like they'd want to spend another week at The Stanley. Dad let them know he was going to take a quick shower and they'd go and find something to eat. After he closed the door, he called back to them.

"Did you guys straighten up the bathroom? Nice!"

Not quite, Dad, Jayla thought.

After getting cleaned up, their dad took them back out into Estes Park to try and find somewhere to eat. They decided as good as the pizza place was the night before, none of them wanted that again.

"We should try this restaurant a guy on the landscaping team suggested," Dad said. "Mexican food. Supposed to be the best in town."

"Do they have tacos?" Dion asked.

"It would be ridiculous if they didn't," Dad replied.

They got a table and placed their orders. As they

waited for their food, Dion elbowed Jayla. She shot a look at her little brother and he nodded toward their dad, who was already looking at the dessert menu.

Dion cleared his throat, getting their dad's attention.

"Fine," Jayla said. "So, Dad . . . do you know anything about The Stanley Hotel?"

Dad looked up from the dessert menu. He had a puzzled look on his face.

"What do you mean?"

"Well," Jayla continued, "maybe you didn't know this and maybe you did and didn't want to say anything, but . . ."

"Just say it, Jay," Dion said.

"The place is haunted," Jayla said. "For real."

"Get out of here," Dad said and smiled. "That paranormal stuff isn't real. You know better."

"I thought I did," Jayla said. "Until I saw a ghost maid in our room last night."

"What?" Her dad looked genuinely surprised. He started to laugh. "You guys are kidding, right?"

"I saw it too, Dad," Dion said. Dion had a serious look on his face that meant he wasn't messing around.

After a handful more "you're kidding me" and a couple of "I don't believe it," Jayla explained everything that had happened to them. She even admitted that they'd been lost in the tunnels below the hotel. To seal the deal, she brought up the web pages she'd found with stories about their "world-famous" Room 217.

"I don't think you meant to do it, Dad, but we're staying in the most haunted hotel room in the United States," Jayla finished.

"For a whole week," Dion added.

Dad sat back in his chair and blew air out of his cheeks. He almost seemed startled when the waiter brought everyone's food a moment later.

"How could you not know this place was haunted?" Jayla asked. "It's supposed to be world-famous!"

"Did you know it was haunted?" Dad asked.

"Well, no," Jayla admitted.

"I don't watch those paranormal shows," Dad said before taking a sip of his soda. "I like action movies and home improvement channels."

"Yeah," Dion groaned. "We know."

"Look, guys, I don't know what to do," Dad replied. "I mean, we're kind of stuck."

Just like someone else we know, Jayla thought.

"I don't think she wants to hurt us," Jayla said. "The ghosts in the basement are another story, but I think Elizabeth is just trying to do her job."

"Elizabeth?" Dad said, holding a forkful of enchilada in front of his face. "You're on a first-name basis with this ghost lady?"

"Yeah, that's her name," Dion said. "And we want to help her."

"Okaaaaay," Dad replied. "I was pretty sure you wanted me to try and find us somewhere else to stay. Or send you home to spend the week with your Uncle Jason or something."

"No, no," Jayla said. "As creepy as it is, neither of us feels threatened. We just feel sorry for her."

"We're going to try and figure out how to help Elizabeth out," Dion said.

Somehow, Jayla thought. *Some way.*

———————

"Do you think you'll be able to sleep?" Dion whispered as he climbed into bed next to his sister. It was later that night, and even with the new information about the ghost maid, their dad was already asleep.

"I'm going to try and stay up as late as I can," Jayla said. She unplugged her phone, happy to see that it was at one hundred percent again. "I want to see if Elizabeth comes back."

"I'm not tired at all," Dion whispered. "I'll stay up with you."

Thirty minutes later, Dion was out cold.

Jayla kept the lamp on for a bit, then decided she'd

have better luck if it was out. She leaned over and turned the light off.

She slid down deeper into the covers, holding her phone underneath the blankets and using her other hand to adjust the pillows. Though she had no idea if or when Elizabeth would show up, she thought pretending to sleep might help make her appear sooner.

It didn't.

Thirty minutes stretched into an hour, and an hour turned into three. Jayla lost track of time and her eyes started to feel heavier by the minute.

C'mon, Jayla thought. *Don't you need to check on the room?*

She wondered if maybe she really was losing her mind. Did she actually WANT the ghost maid to show up in their room?

After another twenty minutes or so, Jayla's eyes slid closed as sleep took her over. No sooner had she slipped into the first few minutes of sleep when a cold wave washed over the room. The frigid air woke Jayla, and for a moment, she wasn't sure if she was just imagining it or if it meant Elizabeth was close.

She's coming!

Jayla opened her eyes and slipped her head

underneath the blankets. She quickly opened the camera app on her phone and slid the mode to VIDEO. With a quick press of the red button on screen, her phone started to record.

She took a deep breath and poked her head back out above the covers, aiming the phone toward the bathroom door. Sure enough, she had a visitor. With trembling hands, Jayla held the camera on the ghostly maid.

Elizabeth was dressed just as she was the night before, in her old-time maid's uniform. Though Jayla could see that the ghost had a face, it was almost opaque and difficult to make out details. She looked at the wall as she had before. The ghost paused a moment, and something inside Jayla clicked.

She was lighting the wall lamp ... or at least where it used to be!

Jayla watched through her phone, keeping her eyes partially closed to make it seem like she was sleeping. She didn't know if the maid even cared, but as odd as it sounded, Jayla didn't want to scare the ghost away.

After a moment, Elizabeth turned and walked back along Jayla's side of the bed. She paused and crouched down like she did the night before. Jayla remembered being terrified that the ghost maid was going to slip

underneath their bed. Feeling a bit braver this time and wanting to keep the ghost in the frame for the video, she squirmed over to the edge of the bed. She lined up the lens so that she could see what Elizabeth was doing.

The maid was feeling around on the ground for something. After a moment, her pale, translucent fingers closed, almost as if she picked something up. A second later, she stood, brushed her apron off, then walked through the wall, disappearing from Room 217.

For twenty seconds more, Jayla kept the phone pointed at the wall where the ghost had gone before stopping the recording.

She reached over and turned on the light. She was shaking, partly from fright, partly from excitement.

It sort of makes sense! Jayla thought.

She looked up at the wall where there might have been a gas lamp. Though it had likely been removed a long time ago, to Elizabeth it was still there.

Jayla realized that turning the lamp off was part of the puzzle. *Maybe Elizabeth didn't think she needed to show up unless there needed to be light in the room! There was a good chance she wouldn't show up at all if the lamp was still on.*

"Why light the room if it's already lit?" Jayla whispered. "She's just doing her job."

She looked at her phone to make sure the new video file she created was there. It was. She wasn't sure she was ready to watch it right away, and instead, carefully slipped out of bed.

When her bare feet touched the floor, Jayla noticed how cold it was. She stepped closer to the window, noticing that the carpet wasn't nearly as chilly. Only where Elizabeth had walked could she feel the cold spots.

Thinking that was another mystery to solve later, Jayla looked down at the floor where Elizabeth had crouched down. The bed cast a slight shadow over the area, but Jayla put her hand where she thought the maid had. It was definitely cold, just like the rest of the ghost path, but there was nothing there. She even used her flashlight on her phone to see if illuminating the area made any sort of difference. It didn't.

What did she pick up?

Jayla pressed her fingers down on the carpet, wondering if there was something underneath it. She couldn't feel anything, but that didn't mean something wasn't there. Obviously, the carpet had been changed a bunch of times since Elizabeth had worked at The

Stanley. She wasn't even sure if they had carpet back then. Maybe there were just area rugs or fancy wood floors like in other parts of the building.

Regardless, something caught Elizabeth's attention and made her stop, night after night.

Jayla knew she had to find out what it was.

CHAPTER 8

HELLO LUCY

When Jayla woke up the next morning, her dad was on his way out the door. He saw her stir and paused.

"Sorry," he whispered. "I was hoping I wouldn't wake you."

"It's okay," Jayla mumbled, wiping sleep from her eyes. Dion was still sound asleep next to her.

"Did your ghost friend come back last night?" Dad asked.

Jayla nodded. "I got her on my phone," she whispered.

He came over to the side of the bed, following the same path Elizabeth had hours earlier. When Jayla picked up her phone, she was surprised to find it was completely dead.

"Let me charge it real quick," Jayla said, confused.

She'd charged it completely the night before in preparation for her encounter with the ghostly maid. But, like it had in the tunnels below the hotel, it seemed to have drained rapidly. *Could it have been the ghost?*

"I'd love to stay and watch what you caught, but I

can't, Jay," Dad said. "I'm running late as it is. I'll take a look when I get back, okay?"

He kissed her on the top of her head and walked as quietly back to the door as he could in his heavy work boots. He opened the door and paused again.

"I left you guys some money by the TV," he whispered. "Thought maybe you and Dion could take an official tour of the place or something."

"Okay," she whispered, "Thanks, Dad."

Jayla smiled at him as he left, closing the door lightly behind him. Then she hopped out of bed to get ready for the day.

Dion stirred as she dug for clothes in her suitcase. A moment later, her little brother was awake, staring at the ceiling and blinking periodically.

"We survived another night," Dion said.

"You didn't think we would?" Jayla asked, confused.

"Who knows with this place?" Dion yawned and slid out of bed. "I don't think Elizabeth would hurt us, but—"

"But what," Jayla interrupted. "Reuben even said there's no way she'd do something like that."

"That's true," Dion said and then stopped halfway to the bathroom. He groaned. "Oh shoot. I was supposed to stay up with you last night, wasn't I?"

Jayla nodded. "You conked out pretty quickly."

Dion was about to speak when Jayla cut him off.

"And yes," she said. "I got it."

Dion nodded. "Cool."

By the time he was done in the bathroom, Jayla was dressed and waiting for him. She held up the money Dad had left them.

"What are we doing today?" Dion asked.

Jayla shot him a mischievous smile. "Feel like taking the tour?"

———

Jayla and Dion headed downstairs to the lobby. The front desk clerk pointed them toward the tour desk where they found a young woman in her mid-twenties sitting behind the counter. She looked up from her phone and quickly tucked it into her back pocket. Pinned to her black shirt was a Stanley Hotel nametag that said *Natalie*.

"Hi," Natalie said. "Can I help you?"

"Yes," Jayla said. "We're hoping we can take the tour."

"I'm sorry, the ten o'clock tour has already left," the woman said. "The next one isn't until noon."

"What about the haunted tour?" Jayla asked. "Can we go on that one?"

Natalie smiled and shook her head.

"We only offer the Night Spirit tour, which is . . ." Natalie began.

". . . at night," Dion finished, reading a sign on the counter. "Plus, you have to be ten or older to go on it. I wouldn't be able to."

"Yeah," Natalie said. "I'm sorry, guys."

"Being young stinks," Dion muttered.

Jayla exhaled loudly and twisted her mouth in disappointment. She glanced at the descriptions for both the hotel and ghost tour, but realized she probably wouldn't get much out of the hotel tour anyway. She really wanted to learn more about the ghosts, and maybe something more about Elizabeth.

She also didn't want to wait two hours.

"Do they talk about ghost stuff on the regular tour?" Jayla asked.

Natalie scrunched up her nose. "Not really," she said. "It's more of a family-type tour, so there's nothing really scary. They talk about the horror book inspired by the author's stay here, but that's about it."

Forget it, Jayla thought.

"All right, Jay," Dion said, tugging at her arm. "C'mon. Let's go find something else to do."

"Hey," Natalie said. "Wait a second. Where are you guys from?"

"Chicago," Jayla replied. "We're staying here for the week while our dad does some landscaping at the parks or trails or whatever."

"I thought I recognized the Chicago accent," Natalie said with a smile.

We have an accent? Natalie wondered.

"My aunt lives out there," Natalie continued. "So you guys are stuck in the hotel all week?"

"Pretty much," Dion said.

"Which room?" Natalie asked.

"217," Jayla replied.

"Oh, wow," Natalie replied. "Did you see Elizabeth?"

Jayla nodded. "We both did."

"You're lucky," Natalie replied. "She doesn't show up for everybody. I've never even seen her."

Jayla pulled her phone out of her back pocket.

"I caught her on video," she said. "I can show you."

She touched the HOME button on her phone and nothing happened. After a moment, she tried it again. Still nothing.

"Is it dead again?" Dion asked, looking over her arm.

"Yeah," Jayla said. "I don't get it."

Natalie nodded. "I'm not too surprised," she said. "Spirits can pull energy from things."

Jayla didn't understand. *Why would Elizabeth or the ghosts in the tunnel try to drain her phone? Did it give them strength somehow? Or maybe they didn't want anyone to see them.*

"Weird," Jayla said and pocketed her phone. "It looked like she was looking for something both times I've seen her."

Natalie nodded. "I've heard other guests say the same thing," she said. "Some people think that ghosts are attached to places or objects. In Elizabeth's case, paranormal investigators think she's sort of imprinted herself into the place, following her routine and doing her old job."

"She straightens up our room," Dion said. "It's kind of spooky."

"Well, she worked here most of her life," Natalie said. "Elizabeth must think she's still on the job."

"It looked like she dropped something though," Jayla said. "And she's trying to find it."

Natalie shrugged. "Maybe she did when she worked here, or maybe she found a spot on the floor that she's trying to clean up. There's really no way to know."

Jayla was quiet for a second. It was hard to tell, but it didn't seem like Elizabeth was cleaning something. Her hand grasped something that Jayla hadn't been able to see, and then she went on her way.

"Okay, well, thanks," Jayla said. "Maybe we'll come back for the other tour."

Natalie grabbed the phone from her pocket to look at the time.

"My break starts in a few minutes," she said. "How about I take you two on a mini-ghost tour?"

"Seriously?" Dion cried. He looked up at Jayla as if the two girls were in on a joke together.

"Sure," Natalie said. "We won't hit all the places, but I could show you a few things."

"Great," Jayla said. "Here's the money for—"

Natalie waved her hand. "Keep it," she said, interrupting her. "I like you guys."

———————

"Let's start in the east wing," Natalie said.

Within minutes, Natalie was leading them through the hallways of the hotel. Along the way, she talked about how the children of the guests were cared for during the evenings on one floor while the adults danced and ate fancy meals in the ballroom.

"And right here," Natalie said, spreading her arms wide, "is the hallway where a lot of the little kids played."

"Huh," Dion said.

"They say if you stand still, you can feel little hands pushing you along," Natalie said. "Want to try it?"

"Sure," Dion said.

Jayla stopped too. They all waited in silence on the fancy carpeting. She listened to try and hear if there were voices or anything. When she closed her eyes, she remembered the voices in the dark tunnels.

"Anything?" Natalie asked.

"No," Dion admitted. "But it's kind of creepy."

"Yeah," Natalie admitted. "It happens sometimes. Freaks people out when it does."

They followed their guide out through the front of the hotel. "This way," Natalie said, pointing to a path to the left that led to a smaller building separate from the main building. "Brrr," she said, starting to jog. Jayla did too. Dion sprinted ahead of them, slipped on the ice but caught himself.

"Hey, did a ghost kid push you, D?" Jayla called.

"Very funny," Dion replied. "Still left you in the dust."

Once inside, Natalie gave them a quick tour of the concert hall. She showed them the large ballroom where banquets were held and orchestras played. She brought them downstairs and into a room and had both of them sit down.

"There's a ghost that lives in here," Natalie said, sitting down across from them. "Her name is Lucy. She was a young, runaway girl."

Natalie went on to tell them that for a while, The Stanley Hotel was closed and fell into disrepair. People broke in and stole things from inside the property.

"Others snuck into the music hall and squatted here," Natalie said.

"Squatted?" Dion asked. "That's weird."

Jayla chuckled, sure Dion was imagining people crouching down inside the hall.

"That means they tried to live here," Jayla said. "Like people sometimes do in the old, abandoned buildings back home."

"That's right," Natalie said. "One of the squatters was Lucy. She was maybe thirteen years old and had nowhere else to live."

"Sad," Dion said.

"It gets even sadder," Natalie said. "Lucy found her way in and lived here for a while. Some maintenance workers came into the music hall one day and found her. They forced her to leave and she had to go out into the freezing cold."

Jayla felt a pit grow in her stomach.

Natalie continued, whispering. "That night, Lucy froze to death outside. They think her spirit has been here ever since."

Before Jayla could say a word, the door to her right creaked and slammed shut. It nearly made her jump out of her skin.

"Hi, Lucy," Natalie said.

Jayla caught her breath and glanced over at the door. There was no one there.

"Is she mad at us?" Jayla asked. "For talking about her?"

"I don't think so," Natalie said. "But she does like to let us know this is her space."

Jayla looked around. "So this . . ." she started.

"Yep," Natalie said, standing up. "This was her room back then. And it still is now."

Dion stood up too. "Yeah," he said, drawing out the word. "We probably shouldn't be here. We should go."

Natalie looked at her phone. "You're right. My break's over!"

As they walked out of the concert hall, Jayla looked back over her shoulder. She glanced up at the fancy window frames, sure she was going to see a ghostly face looking back at her.

"What should I do about Elizabeth?" Jayla asked as Natalie led them back to the main hotel. "Is there any way to help her?"

"Besides keeping your room neat?" Natalie said with a smile. "I don't think so. The best thing to do is leave her alone."

This poor woman's spirit is stuck here, and no one wants to help her, Jayla thought. *If I don't do something, she's going to be trapped forever!*

Once they were all back inside, Jayla and Dion thanked Natalie for the tour.

"You're welcome," Natalie said. "But don't blame me if you get nightmares. Remember, the tour was supposed to be for ages ten and up!"

"Yeah, whatever," Dion said, waving her off and puffing up his chest. "I'll be fine."

Jayla just rolled her eyes.

As Jayla and Dion walked back to their room, they passed another not far from theirs, with a big tray on the floor with dirty plates, glasses, and some uneaten breakfast. There was a chunk of steak near a small pile of eggs. Lying across the plate was a steak knife.

"Room service," Dion mumbled. "Man, I could eat."

It was then that Jayla had an idea. She glanced back and forth to check that the coast was clear. A moment later, she crouched down to pick up the knife.

"What are you doing?" Dion asked.

"I have an idea," Jayla replied. "And maybe a way to help Elizabeth."

CHAPTER 9

FACE FROM THE PAST

"You can't steal a knife like that, Jayla," Dion said as they entered their room.

"Keep your voice down," she hissed, shutting the door behind them. She tossed the key card down onto the nearby table. "I'm not stealing it, anyway. I'm borrowing it."

Dion looked uneasy with the sudden "idea" his sister had. He kicked his shoes off. As an afterthought, he bent down and lined them neatly against the wall. Jayla smiled to see him "help" Elizabeth out.

"What are you going to do with it?" Dion asked, his arms crossed and eyebrows low.

"I'm going to make a little cut," Jayla answered.

"What? On who?" Dion backed away like he thought his sister was going to hurt him.

"Are you serious right now?" Jayla said, shaking her head. "I'm not going to cut you. Just the carpet."

Dion seemed to relax, but then suddenly shook himself out of it. "Wait. You can't do that, Jay," Dion cried. "That's vandalism or something, isn't it?"

Jayla walked around to the side of the bed where Elizabeth had trod the last few nights. She crouched down to touch the carpet. It wasn't cool like whenever the ghost maid was around.

"A tiny little cut," Jayla said.

She wanted to watch the video she'd taken the night before, but her phone's battery was still drained. Seeing that it wasn't going to help her pinpoint where she wanted to make her cut, she tossed the phone onto the bed. She'd have to charge it later. Just then, Jayla had more important things to do.

Dion came out of the bathroom with a small washcloth.

"At least wipe the grease off that knife first," he said, handing it to her.

"Good call," Jayla said. She carefully slid the blade between a fold in the towel, then tossed it back to Dion.

She got down onto her knees and felt around the floor for anything out of the ordinary. A big part of her hoped that she wouldn't find anything. Jayla didn't want to have to cut the carpet if she didn't have to.

After a few minutes of pressing on the floor, Jayla realized there wasn't anything there. She sighed and put her hand down to push herself up to her feet. She felt something under her hand. Jayla gasped.

"What is it?" Dion asked.

"I think I found something," Jayla whispered.

She pressed her finger into the carpet, to keep track of the spot on the floor. Whatever it was, it felt flat and small, but there was definitely something there.

Jayla took a deep breath and pressed the sharp point of the steak knife into the carpet with one hand. With the other, she pulled some of the thick fibers, so that the carpet was slightly off the floor.

With a sawing motion, she made a very small cut in the carpet, popping through the mesh that held it together. Each thick strand broke slightly as the knife's teeth tore through it.

"Don't make it too big!" Dion hissed. He looked at the door to their room as if he expected the carpet security squad to come through at any moment. Jayla wondered if Elizabeth was watching them right now.

Once Jayla had cut a small slit of about an inch, she fished her finger into the hole. She groaned.

"What?" Dion asked.

"There's some foam stuff under the carpet," Jayla replied.

"Let me guess, you're going to cut that too?"

Jayla poked the padding a bit. She could still feel whatever was under there. "I have to," she replied.

Pinching the foam between two fingers, Jayla made her final cut. Almost immediately, she got a whiff of something musty and old.

"Phew," Dion gasped, waving his hand in front of his nose.

Jayla set the knife aside and watched as Dion knelt down beside her. She looked at her little brother, now questioning whether this really was a good idea.

"Well, c'mon," Dion said, nodding toward the slash in the carpet. "Do it."

Jayla nodded and nudged her fingers in past the carpet and padding. Her fingertips brushed against something with a slightly scuffed surface. It felt like metal.

"I think it's a coin, or . . ." She stopped as she got a grip on it. Whatever it was, it felt much thicker than a coin. When she pulled it out, she knew exactly what she'd found.

"It's a locket," Jayla whispered.

Dion scooted closer to look at the small, tarnished piece of jewelry in his sister's palm. It was in the shape of an oval and had a small metal hoop at the top where it could be hung from a chain. Jayla turned it over to look at the back of it. She hoped there were some initials or something engraved on it, but couldn't find any.

"Is that a hinge along the side?" Dion asked.

He squinted and pointed at the locket until Jayla turned it another way. Without saying anything, she slipped her thumbnail into the crease that ran around the locket's edge. It popped open.

"Well, hello," Jayla whispered and took a deep breath.

Inside the locket was a fading black-and-white portrait of a woman with white hair. She wore a black dress with a collar that almost completely covered her neck. A black bonnet covered the top of her head.

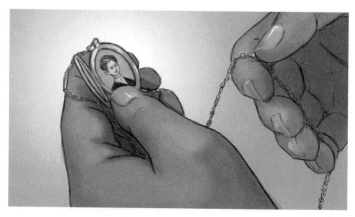

"She looks crabby," Dion said, leaning in. "Doesn't she look crabby?"

"Yeah," Jayla said. "I wonder why. Aren't you supposed to smile for pictures?"

"Is that Elizabeth?" Dion asked, peering even closer.

"I don't think so," Jayla said. "But I'm not sure who this lady is."

Was this what Elizabeth was looking for? Jayla wondered. *Would finding this locket help free her soul so she can move on?*

"What are you going to do with it?" Dion asked.

"I'm not sure," Jayla said, and stood up. "Maybe I should bring it to the front desk."

"Are you going to tell them about the carpet?" Dion asked. He licked his lips nervously. "We're totally going to get into trouble."

Jayla looked down at the small cut in the carpet. She made a few passes over the spot with her socked foot. After a few swipes, it was almost impossible to see.

"I don't think so, D," Jayla said. "I think we're good."

As Dion grabbed onto the bed to pull himself up to his feet, the floor rumbled slightly. One of the pictures on the wall shifted. There was a slight humming noise in the room. And then as quickly as it had started, it stopped.

Jayla and Dion stood motionless, staring at the wall where the picture had moved.

"What. Was. That?" Dion finally managed to say.

"I'm not sure," Jayla said.

She looked around the room, prepared for something else to move. Though she'd never experienced one, she thought maybe it was an earthquake or a tremor. The room remained calm, but a cold rush of air passed by her.

"Did you feel that?" Jayla asked. She turned as if she spotted someone out of the corner of her eye.

"Yeah," Dion said, still frozen in place. "It got cold in here for a second."

Jayla glanced down at her hand, then carefully closed the locket. She didn't like the picture of the woman from the past looking at her anymore.

"I think finding this locket is going to help Elizabeth," Jayla said. "Maybe this is what was keeping her stuck in this room."

"How would that be?"

"Think about it," Jayla said. "Every night, she lights

the lamps that aren't there once the lights go out. Then she stops and tries to get this locket."

"So?"

"So," Jayla said, trying to be patient with her little brother. "It was under the carpet and she couldn't get it. Now we have it and she doesn't have to keep doing the same thing over and over every night."

Dion was quiet and Jayla could tell he was thinking.

"What if she wants to stay here?" he asked. "What if this is her home? You know, like Lucy lived in the concert hall?"

Jayla shook her head.

"She's stuck," she replied. "Like when Natalie said ghosts can get stuck to objects and places. Maybe this will get her spirit unstuck."

Dion glanced at the crooked picture on the wall.

"I don't know, Jay."

———

Jayla and Dion left Room 217 to head down to the front desk. As they walked down the first hallway, they felt the rumbling sensation again. Both of them froze in place and glanced back at their room. Jayla half expected to see Elizabeth come through the door to thank them for finding the locket.

There was no one.

"Weird," Jayla whispered. "Maybe this old hotel isn't as sturdy as it looks."

They continued to the stairs, which reminded Jayla of one of the pictures she saw online. It showed a bunch of people sitting around with blurry figures that appeared on both sets of steps. She tried not to think of it and turned to head down the last flight of stairs.

"Hey," a familiar voice said. "It's you two!"

When Jayla looked up, she found Reuben's old friendly face smiling at them. He was headed upstairs, but paused to talk for a minute.

"Hi," Jayla said. "Thanks again for helping us yesterday."

"Don't mention it," Reuben said. "I hope you guys are staying out of trouble."

Dion elbowed Jayla in the ribs. She shot him a look that could have derailed a train.

"We have," Jayla replied through a forced smile. "But we did find something."

Reuben tilted his head in curiosity. Before she even knew what she was doing, Jayla told him about the locket, leaving out the part about the steak knife and the damage she'd done to the carpet.

"Can I see it?" Reuben asked. It seemed like wherever he was headed could wait.

"Yes," Jayla said. "Of course."

She handed the locket to him and watched as he turned it around in his big worn hands. He popped the charm open and raised his eyebrows at the picture of the older lady inside.

"Oh wow," he murmured.

"I thought it might be Elizabeth," Dion said. "But now I don't think it is."

"No," Reuben agreed. "That's not her. But it could very well be her mother or someone she cared about."

Jayla hadn't thought of that. *Maybe Elizabeth lost the locket with the picture of her mom inside and was trying to find it again.*

"What were you going to do with this?" Reuben asked.

He held it up by the loop at the top of the locket. As he did, it ticked back and forth like a metronome. Jayla saw the old lady's face staring back at her.

"I was going to bring it to the front desk," she admitted. "I thought they'd know what to do with it. Maybe put it with some of the other old stuff down in the lobby."

Reuben nodded. "It was a good thought, but why

don't you let me hold onto it? I'd rather give it to the general manager, David, when he comes in tonight."

Dion spoke up. "Why not give it to the people at the front desk?"

Reuben smiled. "To be honest? David should see this before anyone else," Reuben replied. "He's a bit of a historian and might even have some idea who this lady is."

"Makes sense," Jayla replied. "Yeah, if you think that's where it belongs."

Reuben nodded and closed the locket carefully. He unbuttoned the breast pocket of his dark-green jumpsuit and dropped it inside. Giving it a pat, and confirming the locket was safe, he buttoned the pocket back up.

Jayla couldn't help but feel a wave of relief wash over her. They'd found what was trapping Elizabeth in Room 217, and Reuben would get it to the right people. They'd know what to do with the locket.

"Thanks for letting me know about this," Reuben said. "Now I've got to get down to Room 240. Their toilet won't flush."

"Yikes," Dion said. "One time Jayla clogged—"

"Ooookay," Jayla said, interrupting him. "We don't need to hear *that* story again."

After saying goodbye, Reuben climbed the stairs, then headed left down the hallway.

Jayla and Dion stood on the stairs for a moment.

"You think we did the right thing?" Dion asked.

"I do," Jayla replied confidently. "I bet Elizabeth is already in a better place."

Dion scrunched up his mouth.

"If you say so," he said quietly.

CHAPTER 10

BACK WHERE SHE BELONGS

"You have to be kidding me," Jayla muttered with a look of exasperation on her face. She had left her phone to charge in the room while they ate dinner, and now back in Room 217, it wouldn't turn on.

"What's wrong, Jay-Jay?" Dad asked, taking off his coat.

She pressed HOME and touched the power button on the top. Nothing she did made her phone light up.

"I've had it plugged in pretty much all day," she said. "But my phone is still dead."

"It might be the charger," Dad said. "Or the outlet. Who knows?"

Jayla looked at the outlet. There was another plug above the one for her phone charger that belonged to the lamp, which was working just fine. It wasn't the outlet.

Dion spent the rest of the night watching a movie

that he had seen close to a hundred times. Jayla read a book, and her dad was half-watching, half-looking at his phone, throwing out random Stanley Hotel facts.

"People are saying this place has been haunted since 1911," Dad said, shaking his head. "I had no idea."

Before long, Jayla's eyes started to feel heavy. She reread the same paragraph in her book at least a dozen times, and none of the words seemed to make sense to her anymore. Trying to fight off sleep, she flipped back a page and realized she didn't remember reading that one either. Defeated from fatigue, she found the beginning of the chapter and slipped her bookmark in between the pages.

She set the book on the nightstand and lay her head back on her pillow.

Was Elizabeth going to show up one last time? Or was finding the locket the last piece in the puzzle? Could their ghostly maid finally find freedom from this world?

Jayla closed her eyes for what only felt like a second. When she opened them again, it was almost completely quiet in the room. Dion had fallen asleep next to her, and Dad was lightly snoring on his cot. She sat up and glanced quickly at the alarm clock on her brother's night stand.

11:43 p.m.

She'd been asleep for nearly two hours.

Jayla turned and switched the lamp off, making the room mostly dark, illuminated slightly by the lights outside. She set her head against the pillow and closed her eyes.

And immediately felt cold.

A second later, her eyes were open, and she saw Elizabeth's ghost once more. The maid was headed toward the wall, drifting along her usual path. Though it was the third time Jayla had seen Elizabeth, it still sent chills through her arms and legs.

The maid stopped at the wall to light a lamp that hadn't been there for over a century. She turned and walked back to the spot where her locket had lain hidden for years. Jayla hoped Elizabeth would see it was found. She hoped it would set her free and bring her peace.

Jayla Walters couldn't have been more wrong.

She watched as Elizabeth crouched down as usual to look for the locket. The maid put her hand in the spot where Jayla had made the opening in the carpet and then seemed to pause.

It's gone and now she realizes it, Jayla thought. *Now she can be free!*

Instead, Elizabeth's hands moved frantically, as if desperate to find the locket. Her head turned as if looking somewhere else for it.

Without warning, the maid stood up and stared across the bed with her dead empty eyes. Jayla gasped and slipped farther beneath her blankets. From her burrow, she could see the hazy details of Elizabeth's face: her eyebrows were furrowed, and her face looked panicked.

Then Elizabeth's face contorted and her hands clawed at her cheeks as she silently screamed. Jayla's heart pounded a mile a minute as snowflakes rained down onto her bed. As she watched, the maid continued her silent wail, her dark eyes closed tight. Then suddenly, Elizabeth's spirit seemed to disappear into nothing.

Jayla pulled the blankets down a little to look around. The snow was gone and it didn't seem like the maid had rematerialized somewhere else in the room. Even though she couldn't see the maid, there was still a heavy feeling around her. Cold and uneasy, as if something wasn't quite right.

"Is she free?" Jayla wondered aloud. Her heart beat as fast as a hummingbird's wings.

Just then, a drawer shot out from the dresser along the right wall, landing next to her dad's cot with a thud. He awoke and sat up, just in time to get smacked in the shoulder with another, smaller drawer.

"No," Jayla said aloud. "She's not!"

"What is going on?" Dad asked.

He looked at the dresser, and then at Jayla.

"I made her mad," Jayla shouted, tears starting to stream down here face.

Not surprisingly, Dion was now awake too. He started screaming.

Jayla couldn't stop crying and shaking her head. "I screwed up, Dad. I screwed up big time!"

The room was in complete chaos. More drawers rumbled along their tracks. Shoes were tossed around the room. The cushion of a small green chair in the corner flipped off on its own.

She's looking for it, Jayla thought. *And it's not here!*

Dad grabbed Dion in his arms and put his hand over Dion's mouth to stop him from screaming. Then Dad sprinted with Dion into the bathroom. Jayla followed them.

"How did this happen?" Dad asked, heaving and closing the door behind him. The three of them sat on the edge of the claw-foot tub listening to items in Room 217 being thrown around as the ghost maid continued to ransack their room.

"I thought finding her locket would help her," Jayla said. "It seemed like she was looking for it every night."

"She wants it back," Dion said. "But we gave it to Reuben, who was going to give it—"

"—to David," Jayla finished. "The night manager."

There was another thud outside the bathroom door. It didn't seem like Elizabeth was going to stop searching anytime soon.

"I know what to do," Jayla said resolutely. "I need to go find her locket."

"You're not going anywhere," Dad said, shaking his head. "We sit and hope this passes soon."

Just then the bathroom door blew open on its own. There wasn't anyone on the other side.

"Or we all go," Dad said quickly.

The three of them ran toward the open door and hurdled over the mess in Room 217. They turned quickly, opened the door to the hall, and darted out. As the door behind began to close, Jayla froze.

"The room key!" she shouted.

Jayla caught the door an inch before it closed and

locked them out. She looked around but didn't see the small key card anywhere. Elizabeth had probably thrown it somewhere else. Thinking quickly, she grabbed a small drawer and used it to prop the door open.

"C'mon," Dion shouted. "Let's go!"

If the other people in the hotel weren't awake before, they are now, Jayla thought.

The three of them ran down the hallway, barefoot and in their pajamas. Jayla looked back and could see the door open and close slightly. She just hoped Elizabeth wouldn't move the drawer and lock them out.

I'll make it right, Elizabeth, Jayla thought. *Please don't be mad at me.*

They leapt down the stairs and rounded the corner to the front desk.

"We're looking for David," Dad said to the older woman behind the desk counter.

The lady looked at all of them and seemed confused.

"Well, David isn't here right now," she said slowly. "Is there a problem?"

Jayla knew she needed to step in.

"What about Reuben?" she asked quickly.

There was a squawk farther down the lobby near

the restaurant. Jayla wanted to cheer when she saw the familiar caretaker heading their way.

"Dad," Jayla cried with relief. "This is Reuben. He knows this place inside and out."

"Hey," Dad said. "Damon Walters."

"Pleased to meet you, Mr. Walters. Was that you guys making all that noise up on two?" Reuben asked. "What's going on?"

They stepped away from the front desk, leaving the woman behind the counter looking confused and left out.

"It's Elizabeth," Jayla said quickly. "I didn't think she would, but she showed up tonight and started going crazy. I think she's looking for the locket I found. We tried to see if David was here, so we could get it back, but that lady said he's not, so I don't know what we're going to do." Jayla stopped to catch her breath.

"Whoa, whoa," Reuben said. "Slow down!" He started to reach for his pocket. "David didn't come in tonight. I never gave the locket to him."

A wave of relief washed over Jayla. "You still have it?" she asked. "For real?"

Reuben unbuttoned his pocket and produced the age-worn and tarnished locket.

"Can you put it back in the room?" Jayla asked. "Before she tears the whole hotel apart?"

Reuben smiled and put the locket in Jayla's hand.

"I think you should be the one to do it," he said. "It seems only right."

Jayla took a deep breath and nodded. She knew where it belonged. She was the one who removed in the first place. The real question was: *Would it make a difference? Or was it too late?*

————————

A few minutes later, the four of them stood outside Room 217. People from the neighboring rooms poked their heads out to see what was going on. The door to the room was still opening and closing a bit, as if Elizabeth was thinking of searching the rest of The Stanley Hotel.

Jayla gripped the locket in her hand, her knuckles tight and her palms sweaty.

"I don't know if I can do this," she whispered.

"She doesn't want to hurt you," Reuben said. "She just wants it back."

Jayla nodded and took a quick glance back at her dad and little brother. They looked tired and worried but nodded to show their support.

"Okay," she whispered. "I'm coming, Elizabeth."

Jayla took a deep breath and pushed open the door. Immediately, goosebumps speckled her arms and legs. The room felt cold enough to store meat.

As she made her way to the foot of the bed, the windows started to vibrate as if they would explode and shatter glass everywhere. She quickly reached the spot in the floor where she'd found the locket. With her fingernail, she ran her finger along the edge of the locket one last time.

"Here," Jayla said.

She slipped the locket back into the small pocket under the carpet and padding.

"You can have it back," she said. "I just wanted to help you, Elizabeth. I'm sorry I messed things up."

Almost immediately, the feeling in the room changed. The heaviness lifted, and a wave of relief washed over Jayla. She brushed her hand across the carpet, hiding the small cut she'd made.

A moment later, her dad's face poked in through the partially opened door.

"Are you okay, Jayla?"

Jayla turned around and smiled.

"Yeah," she said. "I am. And I think Elizabeth is too."

———

It took the four of them a half hour to put their room back together. Thankfully, nothing was damaged.

"Thanks for your help," Jayla said as the caretaker headed to the door.

"No problem," Reuben replied, then he chuckled. "The two of you have made my job pretty interesting these last few days."

"It was lucky you were still around," Dad said. "You must work some crazy hours."

Reuben laughed. "That's an understatement. They called me so often that I finally just agreed to move in."

"Wait a second," Dion cried. "You LIVE here?"

"I do," Reuben replied. "It beats getting up in the middle of the night and driving in. Sometimes I think I'm what keeps this place standing."

Jayla thought about that. It seemed like the old caretaker was the heart and soul of The Stanley Hotel.

"Do you think Elizabeth is still here?" she asked.

"I think so," Reuben said, nodding and looking around the room as if she'd appear suddenly. "This was a place that she knew and loved. Probably almost as much as that locket of hers," he gestured vaguely to the floor. "Yep. Even though she's been gone for a long time, this old hotel is where she belongs."

"I think so too," Jayla replied.

The Walters family said their goodbyes to Reuben. When the door was closed, Jayla turned to her dad and brother. She looked a little sheepish. "Sorry for. . ." she stopped, unable to find the words for what she wanted to say. "All of this," she finished. "I just thought Elizabeth wanted to be free."

After the family settled into their beds and said their

goodnights, the only light remaining in the room came from the lamp on Jayla's nightstand.

"Are you going to turn that one out?" Dion asked.

"Yeah," Jayla said and clicked it off.

See you soon, Elizabeth.

AUTHOR'S NOTE

Trapped in Room 217 was a lot of fun for me to write because years ago I actually had the opportunity to stay overnight at The Stanley Hotel in Estes Park, Colorado. Though I wasn't lucky enough to stay in Room 217 (it's quite popular!), I did get a mini-ghost tour very similar to the one Jayla and Dion went on with Natalie in the book.

A big part of our tour was hearing the story of Elizabeth Wilson, who was a maid at The Stanley Hotel in the early 1900s. There are many variations on what happened to her. Some stories say the explosion in Room 217 launched Elizabeth onto the balcony, where she was stunned. Another said that Elizabeth died from the explosion and fell into the dining room where guests were still eating. The one that stuck with me though was where she survived the fall and her hospital bills were taken care of by Mr. Freelan Oscar Stanley who gave her a "job for life." It was said she returned to work eighteen months after her injuries and worked there until she was ninety years old.

As the most haunted room in the hotel, there have been different reports about what Elizabeth's ghost might do during a stay. Guests have reported that she folds their clothes and tidies up the room. I liked the idea that she would light the gas lamp when the lights were out, so I added that bit of information to give Jayla a mystery to solve. I also added the hidden locket as a physical object and the real reason Elizabeth continued to do her job . . . even in the afterlife.

Some of the other creepy things that happened to the Walters kids in the book are based on experiences I had when there. I did go into the tunnels beneath the hotel, but I didn't hear any eerie voices. I also got to hear Lucy's story, and the door to the room slammed shut while I was sitting there! Was it Lucy? I guess we'll never know for sure.

Like Jayla does, you can research to learn more about the history of The Stanley Hotel. If you get a chance, stay at The Stanley some night. But whatever you do, leave the locket alone!

ABOUT THE AUTHOR

Thomas Kingsley Troupe has been making up stories ever since he was in short pants. As an "adult," he's the author of a whole lot of books for kids. When he's not writing, he enjoys movies, biking, taking naps, and investigating ghosts as a member of the Twin Cities Paranormal Society. Raised in "Nordeast" Minneapolis, he now lives in Woodbury, Minnesota, with his awe-inspiring family.

ABOUT THE ILLUSTRATOR

Maggie Ivy is a freelance illustrator and artist who lives and works in the Ozark area in Arkansas. She found her love for art at an early age and pursued it with passion. She graduated from The Florence Academy of Art in 2010. She loves narrative elements and story-building moments, and seeks to implement them in her own work.

DISCOVER MORE

HAUNTED STATES
of
AMERICA

BY THOMAS KINGSLEY TROUPE
Illustrated by Maggie Ivy

A TENNESSEE
GHOST STORY

A MINNESOTA
GHOST STORY

A TEXAS
GHOST STORY